THE JAPANESE TSUNAMI, 2011

I SURVIVED

THE SINKING OF THE *TITANIC*, 1912

THE SHARK ATTACKS OF 1916

HURRICANE KATRINA, 2005

THE BOMBING OF PEARL HARBOR, 1941

THE SAN FRANCISCO EARTHQUAKE, 1906

THE ATTACKS OF SEPTEMBER 11, 2001

THE BATTLE OF GETTYSBURG, 1863

THE JAPANESE TSUNAMI, 2011

I SURVIVED

THE JAPANESE TSUNAMI, 2011

by Lauren Tarshis

illustrated by Scott Dawson

Scholastic Inc.

ISBN 978-0-545-45937-2

12 11 10 9 8 7 6 5 4 3 2 1   13 14 15 16 17 18/0

Printed in the U.S.A.   40
First printing, September 2013
Designed by Tim Hall

TO YUKI, JOSH, AKI, AND MAYA BOFINGER

CHAPTER 1

MARCH 11, 2011

2:46 P.M.

SHOGAHAMA, JAPAN

At first, the wave was tiny.

It was just a ripple in the huge Pacific Ocean.

But it moved quickly, faster than a jet.

And as it got closer to Japan's coast, it got bigger. It grew and grew, until it was a monstrous wall of water, dozens of feet high, hundreds of miles long. It destroyed everything in its path.

The wave smashed into crowded cities, knocking down buildings, swallowing factories, chewing up highways and bridges. It washed away beautiful villages, flattening pine forests and turning rice fields into seas of mud and garbage. In quiet fishing towns, boats tumbled like dice into the streets, smashing into shops and homes.

Eleven-year-old Ben Kudo saw the wave coming as he stood on a street in the tiny village of Shogahama. At first, it looked to him as if a cloud of smoke was rising up over the ocean.

Was it a ship on fire?

But then a siren blared.

Terrified voices shouted out.

Ben didn't speak Japanese. But he understood one word.

Tsunami!

Seconds later, the huge, foaming black wave crashed into the shore.

Ben and his family thought they could race away from the wave in a car. But the water caught them. And suddenly, Ben was all by himself. The wave grabbed Ben and sucked him under. The churning water twisted him, tore at him, spun him around like a bird caught in a tornado.

Terror screamed through his body.

He was drowning!

He fought with all his might, but the water wouldn't let him go. It was as though he was in the jaws of a ferocious monster.

And there was no escape.

CHAPTER 2

7:45 A.M. THAT MORNING
SHOGAHAMA, JAPAN

The score was tied with ten seconds to go. Ben grabbed the ball and dribbled down the court. He zigzagged around guys who seemed ten feet tall. The crowd cheered. As usual, Dad's voice rose up above the rest.

"You can do it, Ben!"

The clock was counting down —

4, 3, 2 . . .

Ben shot the ball.

It sailed for the basket and hung in the air. . . .

Ben's eyes flew open.

He sat straight up in bed, drenched with sweat, breathing hard. It took him a few seconds to remember that he wasn't at home in California. He was at his uncle's house, in the tiny village of Shogahama, Japan.

His five-year-old brother, Harry, had been asleep next to Ben. Now Harry was up, too.

"Scary dream?" Harry asked, putting a little hand on Ben's clammy back.

Ben shrugged off Harry's hand.

"Not too bad," Ben said, careful to keep his voice from shaking.

He never wanted Harry to know that he felt sad or scared.

And besides, a dream about Dad was never a bad dream.

It was waking up that was torture — remembering all over again that Dad was gone. He had died four months ago, in a car accident near the California air force base where they lived. Dad had been an F-16 pilot for the U.S. Air Force. He'd flown dangerous missions all over the world. And he'd died on a California highway, on his way home from picking up a box of doughnuts for Ben and Harry.

A few months before the accident, Dad had announced a big surprise: a family trip to Shogahama, the fishing village in Japan where Dad had lived until he was ten. They would go in March, during Ben's school vacation. They would stay with Dad's Uncle Tomeo; they all called him *Ojisan*, the Japanese word for uncle.

Ben had always dreamed of visiting Shogahama. Ojisan was more like a grandfather to him than a far-away uncle. He'd come to visit them in California several times over the years. Ben had heard so many stories about Dad's life growing up in the village. He couldn't wait to see it for himself.

But not without Dad.

Ben couldn't believe it when his mom announced they were still taking the trip. He'd begged her to cancel, but Mom never changed her mind. "Don't be tricked by that sweet smile," Dad used to say. Mom had been in the air force, too, before she had Ben.

"She's tougher than all of us," Dad always said with a proud smile.

Mom wanted to go to Shogahama. And so here they were.

Harry got out of bed, his Darth Vader pajamas drooping on his bony shoulders. Ojisan's cat, Nya, was asleep at the foot of the mattress. Harry scooped her up. The cat had to be a hundred years old, her black fur rubbed away in places.

She was small and scrawny with a crooked tail that looked like the letter *z*. Instead of saying, "meow," she had a shriek that hurt Ben's ears.

"Eee! Eee!"

Ben wished Harry would ignore the cat so she would leave them alone. But Harry had decided that Nya was a Jedi cat, Darth Vader's special assistant. And somehow the old cat didn't mind being dragged around the house as Harry played his Star Wars games, chasing invisible enemies with his lightsaber.

Now Harry rubbed his cheek against Nya's head and looked at Ben with his bright eyes.

"Will you help me climb the tree after breakfast?" he asked. "I need to make my wish."

Not that again.

One of the stories Dad told about Shogahama was that the cherry trees were magic. If you climbed to the top of a tree, Dad said, you could make a wish.

Ben knew Dad was just telling fairy tales. But Harry believed in everything. For the whole week, Harry had been eyeing the cherry tree in Ojisan's small front yard, waiting for the rain to stop so he could climb to the top. Now the sky was bright blue, and Harry was ready.

"You know what I'm going to wish for?" Harry said, leaning in close. His coppery eyes sparkled. "I'm going to wish for Daddy to come back to us."

The words hit Ben right in the throat.

"Harry," he said sharply. "You know Dad is gone, and you can't bring him back."

Tears sprang into Harry's eyes.

"You'll see!" he cried, turning and running out of the room with Nya tight in his arms.

Suddenly Ben was crying, too.

He stood up quickly, angrily wiping away his tears as he pulled himself together.

Ben had to be tough, like Dad.

During Dad's last tour in Afghanistan, when

Ben was a baby, the engine of Dad's F-16 exploded. He had to eject from the plane over enemy territory. He broke his ankle when he parachuted down. But he still managed to escape into the mountains before enemy fighters found him. For six days, he'd hidden in a cave, until he was finally rescued by a helicopter filled with U.S. Marines.

Ben could picture Dad, standing in the darkness with steely eyes, never once stopping to moan or cry.

And that's how Ben was determined to be.

He went to find Harry. He guessed there was no harm in helping him climb a tree.

But Ben was too late.

He was walking toward the kitchen door when he heard Harry scream.

He ran outside, and there was his little brother, lying in a heap under the cherry tree.

He was covered in blood.

CHAPTER 3

Ben stood between Mom and Ojisan as the doctor looked Harry over. Ben's stomach was still twisted in knots from the sight of Harry lying on the ground. The little guy looked terrible — a blood-crusted nose and a big gash on his arm.

But as battered as he looked, he wasn't so badly hurt. It seemed that the branches of the tree had slowed Harry's fall before he hit the dirt, and that the ground was soft from all the rain. The doctor — his name was Dr. Sato — checked Harry over very carefully. When he was finished, he put his hand on Harry's head.

"You must be made of rubber, Harry," he said in perfect English. "Did you bounce when you hit the ground?"

"I think so!" Harry exclaimed.

This made them all laugh, even Ben. The sound that came out of his mouth surprised him, it had been so long since he'd heard it.

"I just need to fix up that little cut on your arm," Dr. Sato said. "It will just take a few stitches."

Uh-oh.

"Nooooo!" screamed Harry.

Show Harry a cobra and he'd smile and reach out to pet it. But the tiniest needle sent him into fits of total panic.

Dr. Sato wasn't going to get anywhere near Harry, Ben was sure.

Except it turned out Dr. Sato was a genius.

"Mrs. Kudo," Dr. Sato said to Mom, raising his voice above Harry's screams. "Is it true that Darth Vader has a scar on his arm?"

Harry stopped crying.

"Yes," Mom said, putting on a serious face. "Isn't that right, Ben?"

"Totally," Ben answered, trying not to smile. "He got it in a lightsaber fight."

They all looked at Harry, who finally took a deep, hiccupping breath.

"Can I get a scar?" he asked softly.

"If you sit perfectly still while I do the stitches," Dr. Sato said.

Harry held out his arm to the doctor.

"Go ahead." He sniffed bravely.

Forty-five minutes later, Harry admired his sewn-up cut as if it was the best birthday present ever. They all said good-bye to Dr. Sato.

They piled into Ojisan's little car and headed back to Shogahama. The road was narrow, and curved around high rocky cliffs. Out one window, Pacific waves crashed against a wall of craggy rocks. On the other side, the view stretched across rice fields to the mountains, which towered up to the clear blue sky.

"Daddy was right," Mom said. "I think this is the most beautiful place on Earth."

"You should stay longer," Ojisan said.

"I want to!" Harry shouted.

Not Ben. He was glad they were leaving in two days.

He'd miss Ojisan. But being here had turned Ben all soft. He'd been dreaming about Dad every night, thinking about him all the time.

Back home, Ben managed to keep his mind clear.

It wasn't easy. He'd given up basketball, even quitting the travel team he'd worked so hard to make. Hoops had been *their* game — Ben and Dad's. After the accident, just the sound of a bouncing ball would hit Ben in the chest like a bullet.

He'd cleaned out his room so there were no more pictures of Dad. He'd ripped down the F-16 poster that had hung over his bed. When Mom knocked on his locked door, Ben said he was doing homework. When Harry wanted to play, Ben told him to go away.

Sometimes it seemed that Ben had turned his room into a cave, a dark space like where Dad hid after he was shot down in Afghanistan. Yeah, it was lonely in there sometimes.

But at least in his cave, Ben felt safe.

CHAPTER 4

2:40 P.M.

Harry was exhausted from the trip to the hospital. Mom helped him change out of his blood-spattered pajamas and tucked him into bed. A minute later he was asleep, with Nya curled up on his stomach.

Ben was in the kitchen pouring some juice when Ojisan came in.

"How about a walk?" he said quietly.

"No thanks, Ojisan," Ben said with a tinge of guilt. "I'm kind of tired, too."

Every day they'd been here, Ojisan had invited Ben to go exploring. And every day, Ben had thought of an excuse. Ben didn't want to see the pine forest where Dad used to play hide-and-seek, or the marina where Dad learned to fish. He didn't want to hear any of Ojisan's stories about Dad.

Ben slinked out of the kitchen, avoiding Ojisan's eyes.

He'd just stepped into the bedroom when Harry suddenly sat up.

Harry had a dreamy look on his face. Ben wondered if he was fully awake.

"You know," he said softly, "I made it to the tippy top."

"Top of what?" Ben asked, sitting down next to Harry.

"The cherry tree," Harry answered. "Before I fell down, I made the wish, Ben. I made the wish!"

His eyes were glowing.

Before Ben could say anything, Nya suddenly jumped up and yowled. She stood there with her fur standing straight up, then started pushing against Harry's arm with her nose. It looked as if she wanted to roll Harry off the bed.

Was the old cat going totally bonkers?

And then there was a strange sound, a very deep rumbling.

The glass of water on the dresser jiggled.

At first, Ben thought it was fighter jets passing overhead, like at home when a squadron returned to the base.

But the rumbling got louder and louder, and the bed began to shake.

"Ben!" Harry cried. "What is it?"

Dread rose up in Ben.

Ojisan shouted from somewhere across the house.

"Ben! Harry! *Dishin! Dishin!*"

Ben didn't need to understand Japanese to know what Ojisan was saying.

Earthquake!

The shaking got stronger and stronger until Ben and Harry were bouncing up and down on the bed.

Ben gripped Harry as hard as he could so they wouldn't fall off.

It was as though they were rafting on a wild river.

Thud!

The dresser tipped over.

Smash!

The lamp hit the floor, its lightbulb exploding with a shattering *pop*.

"EEEEE!" screeched Nya.

But above all the other sounds was a thundering roar, like the earth itself was screaming with fury. The sound hammered into Ben's ears and pounded his brain.

"Make it stop!" screamed Harry.

But there was no stopping it. Ben didn't know that earthquakes could last so long. The ground in California shook all the time. But never for more than a few seconds. And never like this! Ben suddenly remembered that more earthquakes happen in Japan than practically anywhere else on Earth, even California. In Science, they learned about the earthquake that destroyed Tokyo in the 1920s, and another one in the city of Kobe, in the 1990s.

How could he have forgotten all that?

They'd also learned how skyscrapers in Japan were built to survive strong earthquakes. The tall buildings here were made to sway, like blades of grass on a windy day.

But the buildings around here looked old. Ojisan's house was made of wood and plaster. Like all the houses here, the roof was covered with red clay tiles.

Could Ojisan's house survive an earthquake like this?

The answer came with a *BOOM* that rose up above the other noises.

"Ben, look!" Harry cried, pointing up.

A huge crack had appeared in the ceiling. It got bigger and bigger.

Any second, the ceiling would collapse.

They had to get out of here!

CHAPTER 5

Ben grabbed Harry. He crawled across the floor toward the door, dragging Harry along with him. He pushed against the door. But it was stuck. It was wedged against the cracked, broken floor.

Now what? They were trapped!

Panic churned Ben's insides. They couldn't stay here! But where could they go? His body was frozen. His heart pounded. His mind swirled so that it was impossible to think.

Was this how Dad had felt, when he knew his F-16 was going to crash?

Dad had only recently told Ben the story of the crash. They'd been at the basketball court across from their house. Normally, Dad didn't tell stories about being at war. But something about the *thump, thump, thump* of the basketball had loosened Dad up, got him talking.

He'd described what had happened when the engine exploded, when the lights on the cockpit console had flashed like a video game gone haywire. He was twenty-five thousand feet in the air, rocketing through the sky at five hundred miles per hour. Any minute, the entire plane could burst into flames. His only chance was to eject, to pull the big yellow lever that would explode him out of the plane and send him shooting through the endless sky.

The roof of the cockpit — the canopy — was made of clear plastic, and was designed to pop off when the eject lever was pulled. A small explosive under Dad's seat would blast the entire seat into the air. Two parachutes would open — the first to yank Dad upright, the second to float him down to Earth.

But what if the canopy didn't open and Dad crushed his head? What if the parachutes failed and he fell like a rock straight into the ground? Dad had heard stories about ejections that went horribly wrong. Plenty of pilots had died, or were so badly hurt that they never walked again.

These were terrifying thoughts. But Dad had been trained for these life-and-death moments — to fly through enemy fire, to land on an aircraft carrier in a thunderstorm, to avoid a missile aimed straight for the belly of his jet.

"The fear is always there," Dad had told Ben, bouncing the ball and lining up at the free-throw line. "But you can't let it take over."

He'd eyed the basket and taken a shot.

"You have to choose: live or die. If you let yourself panic, you're finished."

Swish.

Now Ben remembered what Dad had said to him next.

"What you learn in training is to close your eyes," Dad had said. "You breathe deep. You breathe, and breathe, and breathe. And somehow your mind clears so you can do what you need to do."

Ben closed his eyes now. It was hard to fill his lungs — his chest felt as if it was wrapped tight in rubber bands. But he kept thinking of Dad's words:

Breathe.

Breathe.

Breathe.

And somehow his mind stopped swirling. His body relaxed.

And then, almost without thinking, Ben grabbed Harry.

He dragged him back toward the bed, which had strong metal legs.

Ben pushed Harry underneath, and then scrambled in after him.

"Wait!" Harry screamed. "Nya!"

The cat was in the middle of the room, frozen in shock.

Harry tried to crawl out, but Ben gripped on to his ankle, pulling Harry back in.

"Get her!" Harry screamed at Ben.

Ben slid out from under the bed and crawled on his elbows after Nya. He caught her by the tail. She howled and scratched at him, but he managed to pull her back so that Harry could grab her.

Ben had barely made it under the bed when the room seemed to explode.

And the ceiling came crashing down.

CHAPTER 6

Finally the shaking stopped.

It was pitch-dark. Except for Harry's soft cries, everything was completely silent.

"Ben?" Harry said, his voice barely a whimper.

"We're okay," Ben said.

And somehow they were. As the dust settled, Ben could see wreckage all over the floor — broken roof tiles, huge chunks of wood and plaster. The bed had protected them.

The panic started to creep back, cold hands climbing up Ben's spine. His mind began to swirl with questions.

Where were Mom and Ojisan?

What had happened to the rest of the house?

He and Harry had managed to survive the shaking. But what if Mom and Ojisan hadn't found a safe place? What if the earthquake started again? What if . . .

He closed his eyes again and took a deep breath, than another. His thoughts slowed down enough for Ben to remember that Mom had been trained by the air force, just like Dad. She knew how to take care of herself. And Ojisan had built this house himself. He'd know where they would be safe.

Harry huddled close to Ben, crying hard.

"I'm scared," he sobbed. Ben patted his back and tried to comfort him. But Harry was screaming now, worse than when Dr. Sato told him he'd need stitches. Patting him on the back wasn't working.

"Jedi knights have to be strong," Ben said. "Now that you have a scar, you have to be brave."

That seemed to work.

Harry gave a big sniff.

He wiped his nose on his sleeve.

He snuggled Nya close. "We have to be brave, Nya," he whispered.

A moment later, there were footsteps.

"Ben! Harry!"

"Mom!" Harry shrieked.

"Boys, are you hurt?" she called, her voice ringing clear and strong through the dust.

"We're okay!" Ben shouted, trying to sound braver than he felt. "We're under the bed!"

"Stay where you are!" Ojisan called. Their uncle was there, too!

———

It seemed like forever before Mom and Ojisan were able to clear a path through the wreckage. But soon they were in the bedroom. And there was Mom, on her knees, peering under the bed at Ben and Harry. Her face was streaked with dirt and sweat, but her eyes were filled with relief.

"You can come out now," she told them.

Ben pushed Harry into Mom's arms, and Ben climbed out after him.

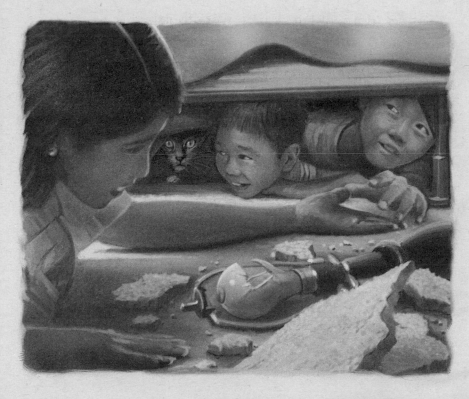

Mom wrapped her arms around both of them. Lately, Ben had pulled away from Mom's hugs. Not now. He could hear Mom's heart pounding through her thick sweater. Nya crawled out and buried her head in Harry's leg.

"That was very smart, to hide under the bed," Mom said, letting the boys go so she could look at them.

"Ben took us there," Harry said, picking up Nya again.

Mom looked at Ben. She reached out and touched his cheek, and he felt a flush of unexpected pride.

But there was no time to talk. Mom found Harry's shoes and helped him put them on.

"Come," Ojisan said, plucking Nya from the floor and handing her to Harry. "We need to get outside. That was a very strong earthquake. It is the strongest I have ever felt. There will be more shaking. It is not safe in the house."

As if the earth itself had heard Ojisan, there was a sharp rumble that brought another piece of ceiling crashing to the floor.

They hurried through the house, stepping over fallen furniture, piles of books, and broken glass. The rest of the house was still standing, but it looked as if it could come down any second. Ben was relieved to get outside. They made their way across the yard and into the street. Some big trees had fallen, but Ojisan's cherry tree was still standing.

"Wait here," Ojisan said. He hurried to the middle of the street, where a group of his neighbors was gathered. Three of the houses on the road were completely wrecked. But it seemed as though everyone was safe.

Mom, Ben, and Harry huddled together in the cold. Harry held Nya tight.

"The worst is over," Mom said.

Yes, Ben told himself. Nothing could be as bad as that earthquake.

But then Ben noticed that Ojisan had drifted to the edge of the street. He was standing with two other men. They were all looking intently at the ocean in the distance.

Ben followed the path of their gaze until he figured out what they were looking at: a strange gray cloud hovering over the ocean.

It looked almost like smoke.

Was a big ship on fire?

No, that didn't make sense. No ship was that big.

A siren blared.

And with a sudden jolt, Ben understood that it wasn't a cloud.

It wasn't a fire.

It was a wave.

A gigantic wave, taller than a building, and so wide he couldn't see where it started or ended. It seemed to stretch endlessly across the ocean.

Ojisan shouted.

"Tsunami!"

CHAPTER 7

There was no time to think.

"Get to the car!" Ojisan shouted.

Mom picked up Harry and they all sprinted to the car and jumped in. Mom pulled Harry onto her lap in the front; Ben threw himself into the back.

Ojisan had the engine running even before Ben had closed his door. The car screeched out of the driveway.

Why was Ojisan panicking? Why was everyone running? They weren't very close to the ocean — it was at least a five-minute walk. Ben had never heard of a wave traveling so far inland.

Probably Ojisan just didn't want to take any chances.

The road had been split apart by the earth-quake. Ojisan had to swerve around the cracks. Ben flew from side to side in the backseat until he managed to put on his seat belt.

"What's happening?" Harry cried, hugging Nya so tight Ben worried the cat's head would pop off.

"We're just moving away from the ocean," Mom said in her usual calm voice.

There was a strange noise. It rose up suddenly, a roar louder even than the earthquake. This time it seemed as if jets were landing right behind them.

Ben turned, and what he saw almost stopped his heart:

A frothing wall of water, rushing up the street.

And it wasn't just water. The wave carried parts of houses, a smashed car, an entire pine tree, slabs of wood and metal. It was devouring everything in its path. Two men were running on the sidewalk. Ben gasped as the wave swallowed them whole.

And now the wave was coming for them.

Ojisan stomped on the gas pedal. The engine whined, and the car zoomed forward.

Mom reached back and grabbed Ben's hand, squeezing it tight. Their eyes locked. At first Ben couldn't read the expression on Mom's face, because he'd never seen it before, not even in the days after Dad's accident.

Mom was scared.

And suddenly there was water all around them, foaming black water, rising up in angry waves.

The car spun wildly as the waves rushed up around the tires.

Time seemed to stop.

The car tipped sharply in the rising water. Ben was held tight by his seat belt. Mom and Harry toppled onto Ojisan, and they all crashed together into his door.

The door popped open. Ojisan fell out of the car.

"Ojisan!" Ben screamed.

And now Mom and Harry were about to fall out, too! The car door was swung wide open, and Mom and Harry teetered in the doorway. Mom clung to the steering wheel with one hand, and kept her other arm around Harry, who gripped Nya.

Ben jumped forward to grab Mom, but his seat belt choked him back.

"Mom!" Ben shouted. "Hold on!"

"I'm trying!" Mom said.

Ben struggled with his seat belt, and finally got it open. But before he could grab hold of

Mom, the car tipped all the way to the side, almost all the way over. Mom, Harry, and Nya tumbled out.

Ben watched in horror as the water swept them away.

Ben tried to climb over the seats, to dive out after them.

But the water was higher now, thrashing the car back and forth. The door slammed shut. Waves crashed over the roof of the car. Freezing water gushed in, surrounding Ben. In seconds, it was up to his chest. Ben tried to open the door, but it wouldn't budge.

The water was at his chin now.

And there was no way out.

CHAPTER 8

The car spun and flipped as it sank deeper and deeper. It became pitch-dark, and Ben got so dizzy he couldn't tell which way was up and which was down.

It was like being in a locked box filled with water or . . . a plane.

A fighter jet that had crashed into the ocean.

Ben remembered the stories Dad had told him about pilot training. It took years to learn to be an F-16 pilot. And the training never ended. There were always new formations to learn, different drills to practice. The worst, Dad said, were the water survival drills.

Every military pilot is trained so they can survive in a water crash. A plane sinks quickly, and fills with water in seconds. Even the best pilot will get completely confused under the water, just like Ben felt now.

And so the air force puts its pilots through practice drills. Twice a year, Dad went to a special training center where he was blindfolded, strapped into a fake cockpit, flipped over, and dunked into a freezing-cold pool. He had to unstrap, find an exit, and swim to the surface — all while holding his breath. In his early years, Dad sometimes failed the test. A rescue diver had to fish him out and drag him to the surface.

But there was no rescue diver waiting for Ben now.

He would escape, or he would drown.

Ben closed his eyes and remembered what Dad had said about escaping from a sunken plane: how pilots turned their hands into eyes, how they would feel their way through the plane until they found a way out. Doors don't work in a sinking plane; the pressure of the water seals them shut. Pilots need to find a hole, or break a window.

The water was past Ben's mouth now, brushing against his nose. He lifted his chin and took a deep breath, knowing it would be his last until he got to the surface. His hands fumbled blindly along the surfaces of the car. He tried to picture what he was feeling — the seat, the roof, the window. He found the window button, but nothing happened when he pushed it. The car's electricity must have stopped working in the water.

Now he had just a few seconds left. His lungs felt as if they were going to explode. He was losing strength. He groped until he found the steering wheel. There wasn't much room in Ojisan's tiny car, but he managed to pull his knees to his chest, and swing his body around. With all his might, he kicked at the window of the passenger door.

Boom.

The window didn't budge.

He kicked again, and again.

Boom.

Boom.

Boom.

CRACK!

Ben gave one last kick, and the glass popped out of the frame.

He turned and squirmed through the opening, fighting the force of the water gushing into the car. He pushed against the car with both feet, and rocketed up to the surface.

But he had barely taken one breath when he was sucked under again.

The water seemed to be alive, with powerful arms that thrashed Ben, tore at him. Each time he fought his way to the surface to take a breath, the water grabbed him and pulled him down again.

He couldn't keep this up, he knew. The water was winning.

And then he caught a glimpse of something big bobbing in the water, just a few feet away. He had no idea what it was. For a second, he imagined it was a whale. Ben threw his body forward, kicking with every ounce of energy he had left.

It was a couch!

Ben managed to pull himself up.

He gulped in the air, filling his aching lungs again and again.

His mouth and nose were filled with the disgusting water. He spit and coughed and blew out his nose, trying to get rid of the bitter chemical taste. He blinked his eyes, which felt as though they had been burned.

Slowly, Ben caught his breath. His vision cleared.

He looked around him, unable to believe that what he was seeing was real.

For as far as he could see, there was water — a churning black soup choked with shredded wood, slabs of glass and metal, and other wreckage.

Ben tipped his head back and screamed.

"Mom!" he shouted. "Ojisan! Harry!"

His voice echoed out, and nobody called back.

There was not another person anywhere to be seen.

The wave had swept them all away.

CHAPTER 9

Minutes passed, and Ben floated on the couch, his face buried in his arms. The blue sky of the morning had turned a dark, bruised gray. The water had calmed, the churning had stopped. Now Ben just drifted along, like a castaway in the middle of the sea. He had never felt so cold in his life.

Or so alone. Ben hadn't even felt this alone in those first weeks after Dad's accident, when he had locked himself away in his room. He had refused to see or talk to anyone, even Ojisan, who had stayed for weeks after Dad's funeral. But in that lonely darkness, Ben had known that Mom was never far from him. There was always Harry knocking on his door, his coach and his friends ringing the doorbell. Ben had sent them all away. But now he understood how important it had been, knowing that all those people were there for him.

Waiting.

Now there was nobody.

A bitter wind blew. Ben shivered. His teeth chattered so loudly that at first he didn't hear the high-pitched sound drifting from somewhere nearby.

Eee, eee.

Ben looked up, sure he was hearing things.

But there it was again.

Eee, eee.

He searched the water. Objects floated by: a lamp, newspapers, a huge stuffed teddy bear, bottles, papers, a soccer ball.

And about ten feet away, something tiny moved slowly on the water, floating on top of a mattress. At first Ben thought he was looking at a ragged stuffed animal.

But then he noticed the z-shaped tail.

And he heard the noise again.

"Ecc, ece!"

Nya!

Before he could stop himself, Ben leaped into the water.

He swam as quickly as he could, blazing a trail through the wreckage.

He reached the mattress and grabbed hold.

"Nya! It's me, Ben!"

The cat stood there, shivering, staring at him with cloudy blue eyes.

"Don't you recognize me?"

He'd gone crazy now, Ben realized, if he was talking to a cat.

A cat that probably had no idea who he was.

But then he saw a kind of flash in Nya's eyes. She limped to the edge of the mattress, and put her nose right up to his face. And she started to purr.

Tears sprang into Ben's eyes as Nya nuzzled him. He felt such a rush of relief, as though this scrawny old cat was a helicopter filled with marines coming to his rescue.

He hoisted himself up onto the mattress, and sat with his legs crossed. He lifted Nya and held her against his chest, the way Harry always held her.

It was the first second of calm he'd felt since the earthquake.

But it didn't last.

Because suddenly the water was moving again. The mattress was being carried through the water, fast. Only this time the water was flowing in the opposite direction — toward the sea.

What was happening?

Ben thought about a trip to the coast the family had taken last summer, one of the best weekends they'd ever had. Mom and Harry had built a gigantic sand castle on the beach. Dad and Ben had bodysurfed for hours, riding giant waves to shore. When the waves lost power, the water would get sucked back out to sea. The current was so powerful that Dad had to hold Ben so he didn't get swept away.

That's what was happening now.

The giant wave had lost power. It was being sucked back into the ocean.

And it was taking Ben and Nya with it.

The mattress plowed through the water, pushing through piles of wreckage.

Think! Ben told himself.

Soon they would be out to sea!

Just ahead, he saw something — a tall, skinny tree poking up through the water. It was his only chance. He'd have a split second to jump off the mattress and grab the tree.

Ben lifted Nya, and put her around the back of his neck, like a scarf.

"Hold on to me," he told her.

He rose up, crouching low on the mattress. Nya dug her claws into his shoulders. But Ben didn't flinch. He kept his eye on the tree, knowing that the timing had to be perfect.

He counted down in his mind, like the numbers on a basketball shot clock:

5, 4, 3, 2, 1 . . .

He jumped off the mattress. Nya sprang off of his back and latched onto the tree. Ben reached out and tried to grab hold. But he couldn't get a good grip. His frozen hands slid across the slippery bark.

And the water took hold of him and started pulling him away.

CHAPTER 10

And then something stabbed him in the back.

He thought he'd been hit by a piece of glass.

But it was Nya. She had her front paws on Ben, and her back claws still anchored to the tree. Nya was trying to hold him in place!

It felt as if ten curved nails were hooked into his skin. But Ben gritted his teeth, and forced his icy fingers to cling to the tree. He swung his legs, wrapping them tightly around the trunk. Bit by bit, he shimmied up, so his body was out of the water.

He'd made it.

Nya unhooked from him, and climbed up the tree so that she was resting on Ben's shoulder.

"Thank you, Nya," he gasped.

Crazy kid, talking to a cat again.

Ben clung to the tree as the water rushed back to the ocean.

It was shocking how quickly the water went away, as if it was draining from a gigantic bathtub. It had to be more than twenty feet deep in places. But within minutes, it was all gone.

In its place was a sea of mud — knee-deep, black, and oily. There was a terrible smell — a rotten, poisonous stench — that burned Ben's nose.

Ben and Nya climbed down from the tree. Ben stared at the heaps of wreckage piled everywhere. There was so much wood and metal, crushed roof tiles, and bits of houses and buildings that had been chewed up by the wave. And there were things, clothes and books and magazines, an armless doll and a crushed baseball cap, a smashed laptop computer.

What about the people who had bought these things, who had worn the clothes and turned those pages, who had played with the doll and looked up basketball scores on that computer?

Where were those people?

Was Ben the only person left?

A dark feeling came over him, blacker than the wave.

Ben had never felt more tired, or more cold. His muddy clothes were frozen to his body. His bones had turned to icicles. His body was raked with gashes and cuts.

His strength was gone. He was out of ideas. He wanted to curl up in the mud. Yes, that's what he needed to do. Close his eyes. Forget all this.

But suddenly Dad flashed into his mind.

He remembered what Dad had told him about his last night in the cave in Afghanistan.

"I was in bad shape," Dad had said.

He was freezing cold, starving, and exhausted. His ankle throbbed, and was swollen to the size of a melon. The cave was crawling with rats, and Dad had hardly slept. He'd eaten some leaves that made his lips swell and his throat burn. He had no water. His radio was out of battery power. He'd been trying to send a signal all week, and had heard some crackling voices on the other end. But he had no idea who those voices belonged to, whether help was on the way or not.

"Things did not look good," Dad had said. "They did not look good at all. But here's one thing they don't teach you in training, that you just have to know in your heart. You have to know that no matter how scared you are, no matter how hopeless things seem, you simply cannot give up hope."

And Dad didn't.

He killed a rat and cooked it for dinner. He kept his mind clear by thinking of Mom and Ben, and the happy times ahead of them. He swung his arms in circles to keep blood flowing through his fingers.

On the morning of the seventh day, Dad woke up to the sound of a helicopter thundering overhead. He was too weak to walk. So he crawled out of the cave.

He made it out just in time to see the helicopter overhead, just in time to fire his signal gun.

Just in time to be saved.

Ben closed his eyes and took deep breaths until his mind felt calmer. He scanned the wreckage for something — anything — that would be useful. He finally glimpsed a can of some kind. It was fruit juice. He cleaned off the top and guzzled down half of it. He poured the rest into one of his dirty hands so Nya could lap it up.

He was still thirsty, but the juice gave him a flicker of strength.

Ben lifted Nya. He held her up so he could look into her cloudy blue eyes.

For the first time he wondered how she had survived the wave, how she'd gotten herself onto that mattress, how she'd made sure someone found her.

Harry had been right about Nya. She was as tough as a Jedi warrior.

"We're going to find them, right?" he said to her, not caring anymore that it was crazy to talk to a cat.

"Eee, eee," Nya said.

Ben decided that meant yes.

Ben carefully draped Nya around his neck.

He turned away from the ocean, and pointed himself toward the mountains.

And he walked.

CHAPTER 11

EARLY THE NEXT MORNING
SHOGAHAMA ELEMENTARY SCHOOL

Ben lay wrapped in blankets on the floor of a school gym. Nya slept on his stomach. They both shivered. There was no power at the school, and it was dark except for the glow of a few flashlights. Ben made out the shapes of people around him: at least fifty of them, laid out on straw mats or blankets. There were very old people, older than Ojisan, and young people, mothers with babies, men by themselves. People spoke in whispers and murmurs. Some were crying softly.

This was where Ben and Nya had ended up last night after their endless trudge through the ruins — to this school on a hill. They'd walked for hours. Ben hoped that one day he'd forget the terrible things he'd seen as he walked: the arm sticking out from under a pile of wreckage, the old man carrying a lifeless-looking woman on his back. He passed a young man sitting motionless in front of a ruined house. Ben went up to him, to see if he needed help. But the man just stared straight ahead, barely blinking, like a statue. Ben waited, kneeling in front of him, but the man refused to speak, or even to look at Ben.

And so Ben walked on, until he finally reached the end of the wave's path of destruction. He saw the school up on the hill, but getting there was the hardest part of the journey. By then, he was so freezing cold that he was completely numb. His feet were bricks of ice. In Health class last year, he'd learned about what happens to a person when their body gets too cold. Their muscles stop working right. Their mind gets all confused. Their heart slows down so there's not enough blood flowing.

That's what must have happened to Ben. By the time he made it to the lobby of the school, he could no longer walk. He'd staggered in, a frozen ghost with a shivering cat around his neck.

He collapsed onto the floor.

After that, Ben's memories were blurry.

There were strong arms that picked him up, soft voices speaking to him, a warm blanket wrapped tight around him. Gentle hands cleaned the mud from his face. Someone put a cup of water to his mouth and Ben drank. He drifted in and out of a kind of shadowy sleep.

The next thing he knew he was here, on the floor of the gym. His muddy clothes were gone, and he was wearing a worn sweatshirt and a pair of sweatpants. Nya had been cleaned off, too, the oil wiped from her fur. There was a bandage on Ben's hand, and more on the cuts and gashes that covered his legs.

People had taken care of him, but he had no idea who.

Without any power, the school was very cold. He shivered under his blankets, glad for the extra bit of heat from Nya's skinny body curled up on his stomach.

Lying next to Ben were a little girl and her mother. The mother was asleep, but the girl was awake, staring at Ben with steady, thoughtful eyes. Ben guessed she was around Harry's age. She had a Hello Kitty doll clutched in her arms. The girl sat up. She reached for a bottle of water, and slid it over to Ben.

He couldn't remember ever being this thirsty. The bitter metal taste of the wave coated his tongue like glue.

He managed to smile a little, but he shook his head, *No thank you*.

He couldn't take any water from the little girl.

She woke up her mother, and spoke to her in a high whisper.

The woman sat up. Even in the dim light, Ben could see the sadness and worry on her face. Ben wondered where the girl's father was.

The woman gave Ben a kind smile.

She even spoke a bit of English.

"Please," she said. "Take. You need."

She pushed the bottle of water to Ben. Then she reached into her bag and took out a bag of chips.

"Please," she said again.

He still had the feeling he should say no, that the woman hardly had enough for herself and her daughter. But he couldn't resist.

At least he knew the Japanese word for thank you.

"Arigato," he said. *"Arigato."*

Ben drank half the water and shared some with Nya. He made himself save some for later.

Then he closed his eyes and drifted back to sleep, into his dreams.

He dreamed of Dad, and this time they were together in Shogahama, walking through the pine forest, running along the beach. And somewhere in the dream, a man's voice called out to Ben.

But it wasn't Dad's voice, or Ojisan's.

Ben opened his eyes.

There was a man kneeling next to him.

"Hello, old friend," he said. "I was hoping we'd see each other again."

It was Dr. Sato.

CHAPTER 12

They sat together in an empty classroom. Dr. Sato had given Ben an apple and a cup of water. Ben devoured them both.

He told Dr. Sato the story about what had happened in the tsunami, how Mom and Harry and Ojisan had been swept away from him.

"They're gone," Ben said.

"No, they are not gone," Dr. Sato said, reaching over and grabbing Ben's hand. "People are scattered everywhere. Have patience. You are safe here. And we will wait."

Dr. Sato had a look in his eye. And for a flickering second, it reminded Ben of the way Dad would look, when Ben would glimpse him in the stands during a basketball game. It didn't matter if the team was winning or losing, or if Ben was on fire or all thumbs. Dad always looked so *sure*. And that look never wavered.

Dr. Sato told Ben his own story — how he'd just gotten to his house when the quake happened. His house was high in the hills, above the school. He'd stood on his porch as the wave hit.

"I watched the waves destroy Shogahama," he said, his face darkening.

It was no use trying to get to the hospital, and so he came to the school.

"I knew people would need help," he said.

People like Ben.

It had been Dr. Sato who lifted him up when he collapsed in the school hallway. Two teachers had helped the doctor clean Ben's cuts and bruises, find him clothes, and carry him to the gym to sleep.

"I hated to leave you," he said. "But some of us went out into the night, to see if we could find survivors."

Dr. Sato looked away for a moment, and Ben could tell that there hadn't been any survivors to find.

Before Ben could think too hard about this, two women came in to speak to Dr. Sato.

They were both sensei — teachers at the school.

The teachers and Dr. Sato spoke, and in the swirl of Japanese words, Ben heard his name. When they finished talking, the women smiled at Ben and left.

"We have lots of work to do," Dr. Sato said. "It could be days before help gets to us. The village is completely cut off. And so it's up to us to figure out how to find food and water. We have ten children whose parents have not arrived. We have to look out for them."

It took Ben a few seconds to realize that the "we" and "us" meant Ben, too.

Dr. Sato explained that the two teachers he'd just met had been here through the night. "They need to go check on their families," he said.

Ben nodded.

"And so I've told them that you will watch over some of the younger children while they are gone."

Ben stared at Dr. Sato.

He was asking Ben to take care of children?

How could Ben take care of anyone right now? How could he do anything when he was so worried about Mom and Harry and Ojisan?

72

But before he could speak, one of the teachers was back. She had three little kids with her. They looked to be maybe five or six years old. All boys.

The teacher introduced them to Ben: Kazu, Hidecki, and Akira.

The boys looked shy and scared. But then Nya stepped forward.

"Eee, eee," she said.

The boys giggled.

Dr. Sato said a few words to the boys in Japanese.

"I've said that you are their sensei," he told Ben. "I've told them that you are in charge."

He patted Ben on the back.

"I'm heading out with some others to see if we can find some supplies," Dr. Sato added. "I'll be back this afternoon."

And in a flash, he and the teacher were gone.

The boys looked at Ben expectantly. He opened his mouth to say something, but remembered they didn't speak English. He wondered what he could do to keep them busy. There was no power, no TV, no video games.

Ben looked out the window at the playground.

And then he saw the hoop, behind the slide.

He'd seen a net bag of basketballs in the corner of the gym.

He led the boys outside, and they all shivered in the cold.

But soon they were running around. Ben's aching muscles loosened up. The sun got brighter in the sky, and they had stripped off their coats. The boys worked hard. Soon the air was filled with the sound of bouncing balls and laughing boys.

After lunch, the boys took a break to climb on the jungle gym. Ben decided to practice his own shots. He worked through his free throws and threes. He was surprised by how good it felt, how much he'd missed playing.

At one point he stood at the back of the blacktop, as far away from the hoop as he could get. He and Dad used to have contests, to see who could shoot from farthest away. The boys stopped their climbing and watched Ben.

Bounce.

Bounce.

Bounce.

Ben shot the ball.

And as it sailed through the air, someone screamed out his name.

"Ben!"

"Ben!"

He turned, and there was Harry, running at him at full speed, his arms and legs pumping, tears streaming down his smiling face.

Behind him were Ojisan and Mom.

Swish.

CHAPTER 13

MARCH 25, 2011
NARITA INTERNATIONAL AIRPORT
TOKYO, JAPAN

Ben sat between Mom and Harry on the airplane. Soon they would take off.

It was two weeks after the wave, and they were heading home.

The stewardess came by for the third time and asked Mom to please turn off her phone. Mom was talking to Dr. Sato. They'd been working together nonstop these past two weeks, trying to get supplies to Shogahama. Mom's friends in the air force were helping.

Finally, Mom said good-bye to Dr. Sato and turned off her phone. She smiled at Ben, put her head back, and closed her eyes.

None of them had slept much lately.

Harry had Nya's cage on his lap. He was giving the old cat one last scratch on the head before he'd have to put her under the seat.

Ojisan had asked them to take Nya home with them, to keep an eye on her. Of course they were happy about that.

Ben looked at the scar on Harry's arm.

"Your scar is cooler than Darth Vader's," Ben said.

"Way cooler," Harry said with a grin.

It amazed Ben that Harry had come through the disaster with no other injuries. By some miracle, Mom and Harry and Ojisan had managed to stay together after they fell out of the car. The water had swept them into the parking garage of Shogahama's only apartment building. They'd rushed up the stairway, just steps ahead of the wave. They'd made it to the roof, waiting there with dozens of other people until the water subsided.

Like all of them, Harry had seen some terrible things. He was having nightmares almost every night. Loud noises made him jump.

Ben, too.

Ben knew how lucky they were to be together, that they were safe.

But it was hard to feel happy when there was so much sadness all around. The quake had been the strongest ever to hit Japan, the fourth-strongest ever recorded in the world. The tsunami had destroyed towns and cities up and down the Japanese coast for hundreds of miles. Thousands and thousands of people had died, and thousands more were still missing. There had been some happy moments at the school, like when Akira's parents finally came, and then Hidecki's. But many people couldn't find their relatives. In the end, it was Kazu's aunt from Tokyo who came to pick him up.

And just when it seemed the news couldn't get scarier, there was another disaster. The quake and wave had damaged a nuclear power station in a place called Fukushima, about forty miles up the coast from Shogahama. Radioactive particles were leaking out of the power plant. Even small amounts of radiation can make people very sick, especially children. People living close to the plant had to flee their homes. For a while, people worried that the radioactive cloud could spread to Shogahama — or beyond.

These past few days, the news from Fukushima had been a little bit better — the winds had shifted, blowing the poisonous clouds out to sea. And life in Shogahama had improved, too. Some of the roads to the village were finally clear, so food and water were coming into the town. Ben was keeping a close eye on Harry. And of course, they had their Jedi cat to protect them.

What worried them all was what would happen to Ojisan.

His house was gone.

Many of his friends were gone, too.

They'd begged him to come back to California with them.

"At least for a few months," Mom had said.

But Ojisan refused, and Ben came to understand why.

Two days ago, he and Ojisan finally took a walk together. They'd made their way into the hills above the school. They looked over at the village below. Ben could see the tears in Ojisan's eyes as he stared at the sea of mud and wreckage. But he also heard the determination in his uncle's voice.

"We will clean up," he'd said. "We will build new houses."

Already there was talk about building on higher ground.

Ojisan had turned to Ben. "The people here will rebuild Shogahama," he said. "We will work together. And we will go on."

We will go on.

Ojisan promised he'd come to visit this summer. Dr. Sato was coming, too. He had a medical conference in California, and was staying an extra week to visit with them.

The plane backed away from the gate and taxied over to the runway. Ben used to love flying with Dad, how he'd explain every detail of the plane, the meaning of every rattle and hum. Ben could hear Dad's voice now, as though he was right there with him.

And suddenly it hit him, a crazy idea: that Harry's wish had come true.

Maybe that cherry tree at Ojisan's had been magical after all.

Because, in a way, Dad *had* come back to Ben.

It was Dad who got Ben through his moments of panic in the quake, who helped him escape from that drowning car. It was Dad's wisdom that echoed through Ben's mind in those dark moments when he was alone in the ruins.

Dad was in Ben's mind, in his heart.

He always would be.

The plane started to move forward, faster, faster, faster.

Harry grabbed one of Ben's hands. Mom took the other.

Ben held on tight.

And together they began their journey home.

A TRIPLE DISASTER

Japanese is a difficult language to learn, and there are many words and terms that don't translate easily into English. One of those words is *gaman*, which means to be strong and patient even when something terrible is happening.

The Japanese pride themselves on their *gaman* spirit, which has enabled the country to rebuild after terrible events — from the earthquake and fires that destroyed Tokyo in 1923, to World

War II, which devastated the country in the 1940s. And it is this same kind of strength and determination that is helping millions of Japanese to recover from the horrifying events of March 11, 2011.

The series of disasters that began that day is known as the Tohoku earthquake and tsunami. The disaster was, in fact, three separate events. Each was destructive and terrifying and could have filled an entire I Survived book.

First there was a powerful earthquake, which hit at 2:46 P.M. under the floor of the Pacific Ocean, about eighty miles from a stretch of Japan's northeastern coast called Tohoku. Most earthquakes last a few seconds. The San Francisco earthquake of 1906 lasted for thirty seconds. The Tohoku earthquake lasted, in some areas, for more than five minutes.

Five minutes!

To get a sense of what this was like, you can do what I did one morning: set a timer and just sit in a chair for five minutes. And then try to imagine, as you're sitting there, that your whole house is shaking, that the air is filled with an explosive roar, and that you are in a state of absolute terror.

It must have been an incredible relief when the shaking finally stopped. Except that the worst was yet to come — a massive tsunami, triggered by the quake.

People in coastal Japan know that tsunamis — a series of massive, powerful ocean waves — often follow earthquakes. If you walk in the hills above Japan's coast, you can find "tsunami markers," slabs of stone built to show where past tsunamis reached. These markers were created by survivors of these tsunamis, and were meant to warn future generations of the dangers of living too close to the ocean in a region prone to these disastrous waves. The markers are engraved with messages: "Don't build below this spot," one says. "Tsunami reached here," says another. Some of these stone markers are more than five hundred years old.

But few communities have obeyed these ancient warnings. Coastlines in Japan, like those here in the United States, are crowded with homes and shops and factories. Like Americans, most Japanese people have confidence that modern science and technology will protect against nature's power. Indeed, Japan has the best tsunami warning system in the world, and in many coastal areas, massive seawalls have been built to guard against tsunamis. Within minutes of the March 11 earthquake, alerts were broadcast all along the coast. Sirens blared. Cell phones chirped. TV stations warned people to head to higher ground.

But the seawalls and warnings were no match for nature's power. In some areas, the waves were more than one hundred feet high. Seawalls crumbled like sand castles. Boats were flung to the rooftops of buildings. Many people tried to escape to higher ground — but the wave followed them. Some of the towns that were destroyed were five miles from the sea, areas nobody believed were within reach of a tsunami.

Thousands and thousands of people were killed on March 11, 2011. Thousands more were injured and thousands are still missing. Hundreds of thousands of homes were damaged or washed away. Entire towns were obliterated.

And yet, when the waters finally retreated, another disaster was unfolding at a nuclear power station called Fukushima Daiichi. The earthquake and wave had damaged the power station. Soon, toxic smoke and steam were leaking into the air. The clouds contained tiny particles that were radioactive — and extremely dangerous to humans and animals. Breathing in a small amount of these particles can make a person very sick.

Two hundred thousand people, who had managed to survive the terror of the quake and the tsunami, had to flee the toxic cloud that spread for miles around the power station. Two years later, most people have not returned. Several towns were so badly contaminated with radiation that they had to be completely abandoned, becoming ghost towns, their streets lined with empty houses, shops, and schools. Decades will pass before the towns will be safe enough for humans to live there again.

Each I Survived book requires months and months of research and writing. Most of the time, when I'm finished, I can almost imagine what it was like for the people living through the events I'm writing about. I could feel the terror of seeing a shark swimming toward me in a creek. I could practically smell the cannon smoke wafting across a Civil War battlefield. I could hear the screaming winds of a hurricane in my mind.

But the Tohoku disaster was so enormous, I really can't begin to imagine what it was like — the terror, the destruction, the exhaustion, the despair.

What I do feel — deep in my heart — is admiration for the millions of people of the Tohoku region and throughout eastern Japan who are rebuilding their towns and their lives, who are determined to move forward, and for the *gaman* spirit that guides them.

FACTS ABOUT THE 2011 TOHOKU EARTHQUAKE AND TSUNAMI

The Earthquake

The earthquake had a magnitude of 9.03. It was the strongest ever known to have hit Japan. It was the fourth-largest earthquake ever recorded in history. It struck eighty miles off the northeastern coast of Japan, under the Pacific Ocean. For several days, strong aftershocks rocked the region, causing further damage and fear.

Image courtesy of *Scholastic News*

The Tsunami

The word "tsunami" is a Japanese word that literally means "harbor wave." A tsunami is not one wave, but a series of waves. The first in the series is often not the biggest. Most tsunamis are caused by earthquakes that occur under the ocean floor. They can also be caused by landslides, volcanic eruptions, or meteor crashes. A tsunami is different from regular ocean waves, which are caused by wind moving over the ocean's surface.

The Tohoku tsunami was hundreds of miles long, and destroyed towns, villages, and cities along more than three hundred miles of Japan's northeastern coast. The Tohoku tsunami was one of the largest ever recorded. On some parts of the Japanese coast, waves were more than one hundred feet tall. The water traveled as far as five miles inland.

HOW A TSUNAMI FORMS

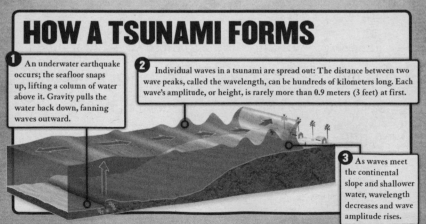

1 An underwater earthquake occurs; the seafloor snaps up, lifting a column of water above it. Gravity pulls the water back down, fanning waves outward.

2 Individual waves in a tsunami are spread out: The distance between two wave peaks, called the wavelength, can be hundreds of kilometers long. Each wave's amplitude, or height, is rarely more than 0.9 meters (3 feet) at first.

3 As waves meet the continental slope and shallower water, wavelength decreases and wave amplitude rises.

Image courtesy of *Scholastic News*

The Accident at the Fukushima Nuclear Power Plant

To help you understand what happened in the Fukushima Daiichi plant — and why it was so dangerous — I first need to tell you a bit about electricity.

The electricity you use in your house and at school — for lights and computers and watching TV — is created at huge power plants. There are about 6,600 of these plants in the United States. Different power plants create, or *generate*, electricity in different ways.

Most power plants in the United States and around the world are fueled by coal. Others are fueled by gas, sun (solar power), water (hydro power), or wind. But thousands of power plants — including the one at Fukushima Daiichi — use nuclear power.

My friend Sally is a scientist, and she's willing to sit down with you and explain everything about nuclear power. But that would take a few hours. So here's the really, really short version: At nuclear power plants, a chemical reaction creates extreme heat. The heat is used to boil water. The water creates steam, which is used to generate electricity.

Usually, nuclear power works well. In fact it's "clean" energy, which means that it doesn't pollute the air. But if a nuclear plant is damaged, things can go very wrong, very quickly.

That's what happened at Fukushima. The quake and wave damaged the power plant and knocked out electricity. Fires broke out. Steam, smoke, and water escaped from the plant. The clouds and water that escaped were filled with tiny particles that contain radioactive energy, which can be very dangerous to humans. These particles don't just go away. There is no way to clean them up. They stay dangerous — some for decades or even centuries.

Statistics of the Tohoku Disaster

- Nearly 16,000 people died
- More than 6,100 people were injured
- 2,668 people are still missing
- Nearly 130,000 buildings were destroyed
  (roughly 1 million more were badly damaged)

FOR FURTHER READING AND RESEARCH:

The Big Wave, by Pearl S. Buck
A novel about a tsunami that hit a fishing village in Japan centuries ago.

National Geographic Witness to Disaster: Tsunamis, by Judy and Dennis Fradin
Tells the story of the 2004 Indian Ocean tsunami, with lots of great information about how these giant waves are formed and their impact.

Sources

Many readers have asked me what sources I use in researching my I Survived books. A complete list of the books, websites, and other sources that I used to create *I Survived the Japanese Tsunami, 2011* can be found on my website, www.laurentarshis.com.

Do you have what it takes?

I SURVIVED

THE SINKING OF THE TITANIC, 1912

UNSINKABLE. UNTIL ONE NIGHT...

George Calder must be the luckiest kid alive. He and his little sister, Phoebe, are sailing with their aunt on the *Titanic*, the greatest ship ever built. George can't resist exploring every inch of the incredible boat, even if it keeps getting him into trouble.

Then the impossible happens — the *Titanic* hits an iceberg and water rushes in. George is stranded, alone and afraid, on the sinking ship. He's always gotten out of trouble before . . . but how can he survive this?

I SURVIVED

THE SHARK ATTACKS OF 1916

THERE'S SOMETHING IN THE WATER....

Chet Roscow is finally feeling at home in Elm Hills, New Jersey. He has a job with his uncle Jerry at the local diner, three great friends, and the perfect summer-time destination: cool, refreshing Matawan Creek.

But Chet's summer is interrupted by shocking news. A great white shark has been attacking swimmers along the Jersey shore, not far from Elm Hills. Everyone in town is talking about it. So when Chet sees something in the creek, he's sure it's his imagination . . . until he comes face-to-face with a bloodthirsty shark!

HURRICANE KATRINA, 2005

HIS WHOLE WORLD IS UNDERWATER....

Barry's family tries to evacuate before Hurricane Katrina hits their home in the Lower Ninth Ward of New Orleans. But when Barry's little sister gets terribly sick, they're forced to stay home and wait out the storm.

At first, Katrina doesn't seem to be as severe a storm as forecasters predicted. But overnight the levees break, and Barry's world is literally torn apart. He's swept away by the floodwaters, away from his family. Can he survive the storm of the century — alone?

THE BOMBING OF PEARL HARBOR, 1941

A DAY NO ONE WILL EVER FORGET...

Ever since Danny's mom moved him to Hawaii, away from the dangerous streets of New York City, Danny has been planning to go back. He's not afraid of the crime or the dark alleys. And he's not afraid to stow away on the next ship out of Pearl Harbor.

But that morning, the skies fill with fighter planes. Bombs pound the harbor. Bullets rain down on the beaches. Danny is shocked—and, for the first time, he is truly afraid. He's a tough city kid. But can Danny survive the day that will live in infamy?

I SURVIVED

THE SAN FRANCISCO EARTHQUAKE, 1906

A CITY ON THE RISE — SUDDENLY FALLS...

Leo loves being a newsboy in San Francisco — he needs the money but the job also gives him the freedom to explore the amazing, hilly city as it changes and grows with the new century. Horse-drawn carriages share the streets with shiny automobiles, businesses and families move in every day from everywhere, and anything seems possible.

But early one spring morning, everything changes. Leo's world is shaken — literally — and he finds himself stranded in the middle of San Francisco as it crumbles and burns to the ground. Can Leo survive this devastating disaster?

I SURVIVED

THE ATTACKS OF SEPTEMBER 11, 2001

A DAY THAT WILL CHANGE THE NATION...

The only thing Lucas loves more than football is his dad's friend Benny, a firefighter and former football star. He taught Lucas the game and helps him practice. So when Lucas's parents decide football is too dangerous and he needs to quit, Lucas *has* to talk to his biggest fan.

On a whim, Lucas takes the train to the city instead of the bus to school. It's a bright, beautiful day in New York. But just as Lucas arrives at the firehouse, everything changes . . . and nothing will ever be the same again.

I SURVIVED

THE BATTLE OF GETTYSBURG, 1863

THE BLOODIEST BATTLE IN AMERICAN HISTORY IS UNDER WAY....

It's 1863, and Thomas and his little sister, Birdie, have fled the farm where they were born and raised as slaves. Following the North Star, looking for freedom, they soon cross paths with a Union soldier. Everything changes: Corporal Henry Green brings Thomas and Birdie back to his regiment, and suddenly it feels like they've found a new home. Best of all, they don't have to find their way north alone — they're marching with the army.

But then orders come through: The men are called to battle in Pennsylvania. Thomas has made it so far . . . but does he have what it takes to survive Gettysburg?